JIŘÍ VOTRUBA

PEPIK

The story of a Prague canary

In a cozy little flat, high above the roofs of the Lesser Side, which is the most beautiful part of Prague, lived a canary called Pepik all covered with bright yellow feathers. Pepik lived with an old lady. The Czechs call a nice old lady a Grandmother. The Grandmother always wore a tight red hat covering her ears. There was no Grandfather, so Grandmother spoke to the canary as if Pepik was a Grandfather.

Pepik's cage was always hanging in an open window while Grandmother was leaning on a red cushion and telling Pepik stories about the most beautiful places of old Prague. Pepik listened and a desire grew in him to see everything for himself, with his own canary eyes.

Once, when Grandmother went to the market, Pepik pushed into the little door of his cage, and it opened! Maybe Grandmother forgot to lock it better or maybe Pepik was so very clever and really opened it by himself, no one will ever know. Suddenly he was outside and flying all alone around the towers and spires of old Prague.

Pepik must have beaten his little wings a thousand times to fly up from his neighbourhood to the cathedral at the Prague Castle. He flew around the spires of the cathedral named after Saint Guy and he enjoyed so much discovering all this beauty with his own eyes, the eyes of a canary.

And what was it down below? Pepik saw doll houses in colors as bright as himself. This was the Golden Lane. The houses in the Golden Lane were as small as the tiny flat of Pepik's Grandmother. But why are the sparrows so angry at me? Is it my pretty yellow color that makes them mad?

Oof. It was no joke to fly so far with little canary wings. But finally Pepik felt like a real grown up. Oh, the Charles Bridge! He wanted to sit down on one of the statue's heads but all the places were taken. Those nasty seagulls!

Pepik landed on the tall tower of the Citty Hall in the Old Town, this was another part of Prague right behind the Charles Bridge. Like a TV camera he could watch the huge Old Town Square lying below. Where are all these people going? From here they seem to be as small as canaries and only the spires of the Tyn cathedral were as high as Pepik was. However, those annoying pigeons all over the place ...

What about a cool lemonade? Well, nobody had offered it to Pepik and yet he was really thirsty after such a long flight. He flew back to the river and savoured its cold water. But what is that strange animal? Oh, oh. It was a narrow escape from the cat's claws. It is so dangerous everywhere. The birds peck at him, the cat scratches him. Pepik started to miss Grandmother.

Pepik found a place for the night on a trashbin in a quiet corner of an old courtyard. But he wasn't able to sleep in spite of the darkness. He was thinking of his little cage and of the safe little flat in his old house.

At daybreak Pepik flew high above the city. He wanted to ask advice from the fluffy sparrows, screaming seagulls and purring pidgeons but nobody told him what to do.

Hey, people, do you know where Pepik could find his Grandmother with the little red hat? When Pepik was completely exhausted an old mailman found him: „Singer-birdie, what are you doing here? The Grandmother with the little red hat was telling me that she was looking for a birdie like you!"

The mailman hid Pepik under his jacket and as he headed to the Lesser Side Square his feet clicked on the Prague cobblestones. At the square the Grandmother in the little red hat was telling everyone how she had lost her Pepik, the yellow rascal.

„But I am here, Grandma" peeped Pepik in tears with his squeaky canary voice. Finally! Grandmother patted his little head, and she was so happy to have her old friend back, she knew she could talk to him again.

In a cozy little flat, high above the roofs of the Lesser Side the canary called Pepik with bright yellow feathers and the Grandmother in the red hat continued to live together. They've both seen enough of he bustling world outside, and when they were looking from their window at the beautiful towers of the city of Prague, they always had a lot to talk about.

... and for all birds living in Prague